A Gift For:

_____

From:

_____

PHOEBE GILMAN
Something from Nothing

Adapted from a Jewish folktale

GIFT BOOKS
from Hallmark

BOK 1092

SCHOLASTIC INC.
New York Toronto London Auckland Sydney
Mexico City New Delhi Hong Kong Buenos Aires

Artist's note:

The paintings for this book were done in oil and egg tempera on gessoed D'Arches satin finish watercolour paper.

Beginning with a colored imprimatura (a thin layer of reddish ochre paint wiped on with a rag) the paintings were built up in alternating layers of egg tempera and oil glazes.

ISBN 0-439-66527-2

12 11 10 9 8 7 6 5 4 3 2   4 5 6 7 8 9/0

Printed in Mexico   49

First printing, April 2004

This edition published in 2004 by Scholastic Inc. exclusively for Hallmark Cards, Inc. www.hallmark.com

For Irving Hirschhorn
Our Uncle
We remember you with love.

When Joseph was a baby, his grandfather made him a wonderful blanket . . .

. . . to keep him warm and cozy and to chase away bad dreams.

But as Joseph grew older, the wonderful blanket grew older too.

One day his mother said to him, "Joseph, look at your blanket. It's frazzled, it's worn, it's unsightly, it's torn. It is time to throw it out."

"Grandpa can fix it," Joseph said.
Joseph's grandfather took the blanket and turned it round and round.

"Hmm," he said as his scissors went snip, snip, snip and his needle flew in and out and in and out, "There's just enough material here to make . . ."

. . . a wonderful jacket. Joseph put on the wonderful jacket and went outside to play.

But as Joseph grew older, the wonderful jacket grew older too.

One day his mother said to him, "Joseph, look at your jacket. It's shrunken and small, doesn't fit you at all. It is time to throw it out!"

"Grandpa can fix it," Joseph said.
Joseph's grandfather took the jacket and turned it round and round.

"Hmm," he said as his scissors went snip, snip, snip
and his needle flew in and out and in and out,
"There's just enough material here to make . . ."

. . . a wonderful vest. Joseph wore the wonderful vest
to school the very next day.

But as Joseph grew older, the wonderful vest grew
older too.

מזל טוב

One day his mother said to him, "Joseph, look at your vest! It's spotted with glue and there's paint on it too. It is time to throw it out!"

"Grandpa can fix it," Joseph said.
Joseph's grandfather took the vest and turned it round and round.

"Hmm," he said as his scissors went snip, snip, snip and his needle flew in and out and in and out, "There's just enough material here to make . . ."

. . . a wonderful tie. Joseph wore the wonderful tie to his grandparents' house every Friday.

But as Joseph grew older, his wonderful tie grew older too.

One day his mother said to him, "Joseph, look at your tie! This big stain of soup makes the end of it droop. It is time to throw it out!"

"Grandpa can fix it," Joseph said.
Joseph's grandfather took the tie and turned it
round and round.

"Hmm," he said as his scissors went snip, snip, snip and his needle flew in and out and in and out, "There's just enough material here to make . . ."

. . . a wonderful handkerchief. Joseph used the wonderful handkerchief to keep his pebble collection safe.

But as Joseph grew older, his wonderful handkerchief grew older too.

One day his mother said to him, "Joseph, look at your handkerchief! It's been used till it's tattered, it's splotched and it's splattered. It is time to THROW IT OUT!"

"Grandpa can fix it," Joseph said.
Joseph's grandfather took the handkerchief and
turned it round and round.

"Hmm," he said as his scissors went snip, snip, snip
and his needle flew in and out and in and out,
"There's just enough material here to make . . ."

21

. . . a wonderful button. Joseph wore the wonderful button on his suspenders to hold his pants up.

One day his mother said to him, "Joseph, where is your button?"
Joseph looked. It was gone!

He searched everywhere but he could not find it.
Joseph ran down to his grandfather's house.

24

"My button! My wonderful button is lost!"
His mother ran after him. "Joseph! Listen to me.

"The button is gone, finished, kaput. Even your grandfather can't make something from nothing." Joseph's grandfather shook his head sadly. "I'm afraid that your mother is right," he said.

The next day Joseph went to school. "Hmm," he said, as his pen went scritch scratch, scritch scratch, over the paper. "There's just enough material here to make . . ."

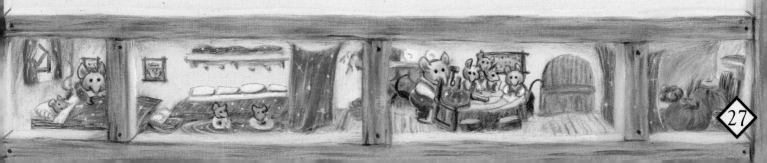

. . . a wonderful story.